I0633453

It's Time

Flash Fiction by

Katie Sullivan Hughbanks

Finishing Line Press
Georgetown, Kentucky

It's Time

ACKNOWLEDGMENTS

Kentucky Monthly: "His Sunset", "Lock and Key", "And Then There Were Three", "A
Perfect Pinecone"
Dodging the Rain (Ireland): "Flight" and "Secrets"
Ignatian Literary Magazine: "The Blossom Shop, 1982"
Heartland Society of Women Writers: "Sparkle"
LEO Weekly: "The Time Capsule"

Publisher: Leah Huete de Maines
Editor: Christen Kincaid
Cover Art: Katie Sullivan Hughbanks
Author Photo: Jenny Cobb
Cover Design: Elizabeth Maines McCleavy

Order online: www.finishinglinepress.com
also available on amazon.com

Author inquiries and mail orders:
Finishing Line Press
PO Box 1626
Georgetown, Kentucky 40324
USA

Contents

Epigraph.. 1

The Blossom Shop, 1982 2

His Sunset 6

Flight 8

Secrets 9

And Then There Were Three.. 11

A Perfect Pinecone 13

Sparkle... 15

Saw Dust 16

Fifth-Grade Project 18

Lock and Key... 20

Independence.. 22

The Time Capsule... 24

To Jenny and David, their birth mothers, and all the women who have made hard choices. Even untold stories can be beautiful and teach us about human goodness.

Epigraph:

it is time:
join the peonies and shake with laughter,
sway beside grape vines
with tendrils dancing in May wind;
dress like lacy ferns in verdant frills
and console the despairing azure sky,
so blue blue blue.

the chickadee speaks in black and white,
now, my friend.

so leave open the windows and
the doors unbarred.
the fields, the forests, fresh air—
they are waiting for each of us.

come, let us go!

The Blossom Shop, 1982

A bell above the door jingled, announcing Mark's entrance to the shop. The din of rain and traffic outside hushed as the door stuttered shut, and a peculiar combination of eucalyptus and lilies greeted him, the scents taking up the space of the tiny store. He lowered the soggy newspaper he held over his head, brown hair glistening with wayward raindrops. The tall man paused at the doorway to shake off his long raincoat and allow his eyes to adjust to the shop's nominal lighting.

A dumpy florist shop this is, he thought and looked at his wristwatch. *Better make this quick. Quarter till six. She'll be waiting.*

Quickly he scanned the store, tall ceilings needing paint and dim lights that made Mark squint. Silk floral arrangements decorated shelves to the right; fresh-cut flowers of all kinds waited in glass-front refrigerators across the back wall. To the left was a counter cluttered with florist shop accoutrements— ribbon, floral tape, scissors. Behind the counter was empty—no clerk about, no movement at all.

"Where the hell is somebody to help me?" he mumbled lowly. He could almost hear his watch ticking away the seconds. *Must get there by 6:15. With flowers or not. She's waiting, and here I go screwing it all up.*

In only a half an hour, he'd be in Sheila's arms. They'd have time for a quick dinner and then who knew what. His shaven cheeks flushed warm at the thought. *Sheila.* They met at a conference in Columbus, hit it off immediately, exchanged work phone numbers (not home phone numbers, certainly). She called yesterday to say she'd be in town for the night, would love to see Mark if he could get away.

Get away. That was not a problem. Tuesday is Clare's bunco night. She'd be out till 10. Mark had never in their 12 years together done anything remotely like this. He could get away, but would he get away with it? His heart quickened at the thought.

I better hurry. I'll never make it if I don't go now. Mark turned to leave the tiny florist shop, but behind him he heard a shuffling. Someone was coming out of the back room.

In a breath, he called out. "Hello? Could I get some help here?"

Slowly a small woman in a stained apron approached the messy counter.

"Here I am. Sorry you had to wait," she croaked. She seemed half his size, shoulders bent over, her frame fragile. Her gray hair matched her gray eyes. Like her store, everything about this clerk seemed old. She appraised the man in front of her and asked, "What can I do for you?"

"I'm in a hurry and need a gift for, uh, for a friend. I want to give her flowers to make her feel, well, *special.*"

"I see." And she did. She saw his clean jawline, the tie at his neck not loosened after work. The color on his face, his red ears. She saw.

"First, let me take that wet newspaper for you." She reached for the paper he had used as an umbrella and gently grasped it at a corner. "Looks like this is old news now." She chuckled almost imperceptibly as she shuffled to a garbage can behind the counter.

"Now, what would this *lady* like?" the clerk inquired.

Mark stole a look at the silk flower arrangements bunched together in vases and pots on the closest shelf. He lifted a vase of mauve and blue flowers. "These are pretty. She'd like these, maybe."

"They are nice," the woman agreed. "You don't see mauve and blue flowers much in the natural world. Seems to me they are a little artificial. Well, more than a little, really. They *are* silk."

The man frowned. "Are you saying ladies don't like artificial flowers? Is that right?"

"Not saying that directly, no sir, but fake is fake, if you ask me." She looked at him, her gray eyes offering kindness. "These silk flowers will last and last. They will probably hang around longer than you or me or your lady friend, honestly."

He nodded a little self-righteously. "Yes, they will last. She'll remember me with those flowers. How much are they?" He reached for his wallet.

"OK, if you want them, I will sell them to you, but are you sure your friend likes blue and mauve?"

"Well, I don't really know. Most women do, right?"

"I can't speak for most women, sir. The ladies who come into my shop most often buy cut flowers. You know, sunflowers to brighten a kitchen. Carnations because they are a good bargain and stay fresh a long time. Sometimes roses. A lot of 'em like statice flowers because they're pretty purple even after they dry up."

Dismayed, Mark gave in. He set the vase back on the shelf with the other silk arrangements. "OK, I'll take a bouquet—you pick out the flowers, just make it quick. I'm supposed to meet her in a few minutes."

Outside, the church bell across the street began its hourly tune. "Six o'clock. I really need to go. Do you have a bouquet that's already made? I need to get there."

The clerk took a breath and closed her eyes for a few seconds. When she opened them, she saw a wet, angry man ready to either pounce at her for delaying him or turn around and bolt from her shop. She reached across the counter and touched his coat sleeve. "Sir, I know you're in a rush, but can I please show you a third option?"

Mark hesitated. *Sheila*, his mind teetered. He thought of her blond hair, the red dress she wore that day at the conference. *Sheila*. The old woman still had her hand on his arm. He relented. "OK, show me."

She led him past the silk flowers toward a corner of the shop. His tall body followed her tiny one. Light from the display window made this corner brighter than the rest of the store. "Look at that," she whispered. "The rain is slowing. Looks like the clouds'll be breaking up soon."

Mark nodded, his impatience somehow falling away.

"Here, sir." The lady motioned to a series of shelves with potted plants. "Now these will last, too. Maybe not as long as those silk flowers, but they could be around for years, even decades if they're treated right."

"But they're not flowers. I wanted to get Sheila flowers."

"Oh, many of these *will* flower. They just have to mature first. And when one creates a blossom, it will be special, *really* special. You see, with one of these plants, your gal can get the best of both worlds—a decoration that will endure and a chance to nurture and care for it. Like this one. It's a pothos. It will last who knows, five, maybe ten years. People say it symbolizes luck, but I don't know. It's awfully nice."

4

Mark touched a shiny green leaf and studied the plants along the shelves. The clerk smiled, then held out her hand to another plant, one with heart-shaped leaves. "What about this one? It's a philodendron. Grows and grows. Doesn't need a lot of fuss, just water every week or so and a bit of sunlight. It's not flashy red or bright blue, but it'll stay green for the longest time. Philodendron plants can last twenty years or more. They say they can even purify the air around them. How about that? This plant'll be helpful as well as pass the test of time. And you know, 'philo' means 'love'. A perfect gift for a woman you love."

Love? I don't love Sheila. I don't even know her. Mark's stomach turned and suddenly he felt sick.

"I know you are in a hurry. You want to go with the philodendron, sir?"

"I'd, I'd...I'd like the philodendron, yes." He moved to the counter, slipped a bill out of his wallet.

"Should I put it in a bag? Or I have a box in the back room. Don't want any dirt getting on your nice raincoat."

Mark stopped her abruptly. "I don't need a bag." He handed the woman the bill but hesitated to let go. His brown eyes met her gray. "Thank you, ma'am. You have been a big help. I'm sorry if I was curt with you." He let go of the bill and nodded. "Really. Thank you."

The woman didn't speak but watched Mark leave. Going out the door, he checked his wristwatch again. Her hearing was as old as the rest of her, but she listened for the church bell to chime 6:30. Instead, she was pretty certain she heard him mutter to himself, "If I rush, I can get home and give this to Clare before she leaves for bunco." The man stepped out onto the sidewalk, leafy vines dangling hopefully from his hands.

His Sunset

We had been climbing all afternoon, my father and me. With Mom gone for six years now and my brothers moved away, Dad said he had just one dream left before his time was up—to climb the Pinnacle, a mountain that looks over our little town. Most men here have climbed the mountain a hundred times, camped there as boys, made out with girls at the top as teenagers. Not Dad. He'd never been on the Pinnacle once. But then, Dad has been blind from birth.

That Saturday, we—Dad and I—climbed that craggy little mountain. After the grueling ascent, Dad's fragile hand in mine the whole way to lead him up the trail, we had finally arrived at the top. The warmth of the afternoon sun was beginning to fade as evening approached. The climb had taken nearly three hours—usually just over a thirty-minute hike for me alone. And finally, we had reached the crest overlooking a corner of Kentucky. We both were thirsty, worn, feeling ragged, but there.

Atop the Pinnacle, I helped him bend to sit on a piece of shelf rock that watches over the valley below. From here, I could see Dad's little farmhouse— where my brothers and I were born, where we grew up, where my mother had shriveled away to nothing in her last few years, and where Dad, I knew, would pass on to be with Mom. And from here—or anywhere—Dad couldn't see a thing.

Taking in the vista, I stood next to the rock he sat on, his cane lazily leaning against a tree. A sense of satisfaction washed over me, happy that I had gotten him this far—my blind dad on this mountain. Looking out at the evening sky and the miles of land in front of us, I couldn't help but sigh. Then Dad spoke quietly, softly among the evening songbirds. "Tell me, Laurel. What does it look like? Out there. What does it look like?" I heard a wince of desperation in his voice, the pain of his not knowing, of him being left out—an isolation that had lasted a lifetime, his lifetime. In a moment, he asked again, "What does it look like?"

"Well, Dad," I hesitated, trying to think fast. After a pause, I tried. "It's like Mom's hands when I was little."

"Huh?" he asked, exhaustion and confusion in his voice.

I paused and then spoke in a whisper, my words dancing quietly with the breeze. I took my father's hand in mine and placed his fingers on the center of my palm. "Soft and smooth, Dad. The colors, the shades—they're soft and smooth like her hands were. The sun is like her palm, round and warm, delicate flesh. Fresh. Real. The edges of the sky are tipped in different colors, like her fingers spread outward, her long fingertips stretching out to the sky, reaching for nighttime, reaching for peace, spreading peace." I moved his hand to feel my own fingertips with his. He gently touched each of my fingers. "The rays, the colors of the sun, they offer comfort, just like Mom's touch did. Feel it on your cheeks, Dad; it's as if Mom is right here."

Was this enough to satisfy him? Could he see this sunset with my words, with his hands?

Dad took in a deep breath, then let it go. His quiet, calm voice rose up to me standing above him. "Yes, Laurel, I see it. I feel it. The sunset is your mother's hands. A rare beauty, indeed, Laurel. A rare and elegant beauty." His words hung in the air like the leaves fluttering in the maples and oaks around us.

He could not see my smile that surely revealed the pride and gratitude I felt just then for my father, for the memory of my mother, for the world in front of me. Perhaps when he heard me sniffle, he knew what it was all about.

In no time, though, Dad's old-man voice broke my sentimentality. "Guess we better go back now. I'm hungry as hell from the climb up here, and you'll need to be getting home to William and the girls."

My father and I, we had reached the top of the Pinnacle, and it was time to begin our arduous hike back down. Night was beginning to fall, and it would be dangerous to dally any longer.

For me, the darkness was coming soon, but for Dad, darkness was not among his worries. I suppose that day Daddy saw a different light, a sunset in the palm of his hand. It was a light he could carry with him down the mountain and back home.

Flight

Ten silent birds fly in formation in a sapphire sky as new recruits march in rows. Late November, but the uniformed figures in camouflage are in the spring of life—young, muscled, healthy. Slender and acne-faced, he steps in time with his comrades.

Nine months into his army career, Peterson gets his orders to join the conflict across the blue Pacific. Excitement and trepidation ensue.

Eight letters to his mother, every Sunday for two months, assure her he is managing. *The war in Vietnam is practically over anyhow,* he writes. *I miss your brownies,* he writes. *Do you think the Reds stand a chance this season?* he writes.

Seven days a week he trudges with swampy water in his boots and slaps at insect bites covering his skin. He remains wet, hot, filthy.

Six planes fly in on that fateful Thursday, bringing more troops and even more guns. The C-97s drop their cargo and leave, propellers barely having a moment to come to a rest before spinning the planes forward again.

Five buddies along with Peterson become lost in the jungle while delivering supplies. Gunfire rings out around them, past their ears, in front of their eyes.

Four muddied men circle the redhead, Thompson, as he gropes his chest, blood erupting in a vermillion poppy flower against his olive t-shirt. His breaths come urgently; he is drowning in the crimson.

Three blasts boom suddenly—three bombs explode—three men scream and run.

Two thin eyes appear and peer at Peterson's face as he holds the fiery flesh of his thigh. His body writhes on the muddy ground. Hit by mortar and in infernal pain, he watches in terror at the enemy soldier above him.

One thunderous bullet to the forehead takes his life in the sweltering rice paddy and a stillness falls over the land. No movement through the brush, no stirring on the earth, except—

Ten silent birds fly in formation above, in a sapphire sky.

Secrets

She lay in the hospital bed, gray walls surrounding her gray face.

Panic struck her, and her already wrinkled brow took on even deeper grooves as she worried silently. Beside her bed, an elderly man sat huddled over her moribund body, eyes closed, his ancient hands held a string of black beads clasped in prayer over her.

I'm dying, she thought through her pain. *Now. I am going. Soon—now. This is the last chance.* She battled in her mind as her body was losing its war with cancer. *Tell him or not?* She knew she had to choose and choose immediately. Death would keep her secret if she waited any longer.

With great effort, Martha opened her eyelids. William stared into her foggy eyes, pleading for her to stay. "Martha, sweetheart, you know I love you," his gravelly voice choked. "I haven't been perfect, but I tried to be a good husband. I love you so much, Martha." His voice faded.

The old woman nodded gently, almost imperceptibly. With concentrated effort, she reached for her husband's wrist. The rosary in his hand fell to the floor. He bent to retrieve it, then looked into her eyes. He gaped, incredulous. It was impossible to believe she was going, yet he knew she was.

He leaned in close as she opened her mouth, a mouth he had known for decades, the lips he kissed each morning and night. "Will, I—I—love you," her quiet voice sputtered. "But—but—I need to tell…" Her words dropped off.

Perhaps speaking was too much. Perhaps her energy was too little. Perhaps even trying to tell him would steal away her last breaths. She looked at the black beads he held.

With every bit of strength she could muster in her sick, frail body, she continued through raspy, shallow gasps. "Will, I—I—I wasn't," her white head bent, "faithful. I wasn't always faithful to you." Tears fell from her gray eyes. "Once. A boss, years ago. Ken. In charge of purchasing. It was only once. It was a terrible choice. After the second miscarriage. I knew it was wrong. It was my secret, but I—I still loved you and love you now." Tears spilled onto creased cheeks. "I'm sorry."

William shook his head, first in confusion, then in disbelief. Ken? He didn't recall any boss she had had, and certainly not one named Ken. Unfaithful?

Slowly, the image of a man with a red beard and a hearty laugh—a laugh too loud, too bold, came to mind. No, that wasn't a Ken. That was Mark. Or Mike. Not Ken. She had been unfaithful? Martha?

He had no time to think.

Setting the rosary on her blanket, he reached for her hand in desperation. Tears pricked at his old eyes; determination livened his weak voice. "I knew, Martha. I knew then and I still loved you. Still love you now. It's OK, just stay a little longer. You are forgiven. You were forgiven even back then. It didn't matter. We had each other."

Her final breath. Silence.

Tears flowed freely down the old man's face as he held his head in his hands. After a moment, he looked at his wife's still face, saw peace rest on her pale cheeks. On the hospital blanket, dark beads glistened in the fluorescent lighting; the crucifix lay face up.

"I told you a lie," he whispered to his wife's body. "My last words to you were not the truth. I didn't know; I hadn't known. I never even suspected." In silence, he pressed a button to bring the nurse into the room, to pronounce his Martha dead, to make it all official.

Then he sat surrounded by gray walls and waited beside his wife. She had died the way she'd hoped—with no secrets, nothing between them but the truth.

Will, gray faced, lifted the rosary in his rough hand. With a shudder, he realized he would not be so lucky. He would, when the time comes, take his secret, his lie, to the grave.

And Then There Were Three

As I pass by Room 202, I am a tangled web of feelings. Even now, when I help deliver a newborn, I am shocked how profoundly it affects me. In the hallways and in these rooms, I walk with my head high with a smile for every person, appearing confident and comfortable in these blue scrubs. But today, once again, I am a mess inside, watching two people become three.

Jonathan was my third love, the one I married. My first love was cross country, which I discovered when I was a leggy colt my freshman year at Campbell County High School. Running was all I cared about until my senior year when I discovered my second love: medicine. Mrs. Smith's anatomy class was challenging but inspiring, and when I graduated, I headed straight to nursing school. Only after I finished my clinicals did I meet the tall, dark-eyed man who would become my husband. We had run side by side in a 10K race one county over, strangers chatting, flirting as we competed. I won my age group; he won my heart. He lit up my world in a way I could not have imagined, and his love made my life complete.

But today, as I pass by Room 202, little seems complete anymore. Beyond that hospital room door, a lovely woman my age—31—looks radiant despite sitting up in a hospital bed, having given birth a few hours ago. Her blond hair flows down her shoulders and spills over the pillow where she rests. In a chair next to the bed sits a man who vaguely resembles my Jonathan—dark eyes but hair a bit longer than Johnny's. His knees push up against the bed's mattress, and he leans forward, trying to be as close as possible to his wife, as if they are physically connected. On his lap, wrapped in a pink blanket I retrieved from the neonatal wing's supply closet, is the most beautiful infant I have ever seen. She is perfect with skin like porcelain, her hair, gold-white swan feathers. Delicate as rose petals, as flawless as a newly-discovered pearl. When the head delivery nurse handed that child to me in the birthing room, I could barely stand myself for the jealousy that rumbled in my chest. As I wiped the little girl's face and hands and feet with warm toweling, cleaning and examining her, I thought of the gifts life brings; strange that I was reminded, too, of the cruelty life can bestow.

Yes, life can be harsh; nature can be brutal. The last three and a half years have proven that to me. My Jonathan is gone—he fought like a champion, but the brain cancer took him in just nine months. My light, my love has been gone over two years. With him, the cancer took my dreams. The loss is double: I lost my husband and my future children. I am destined to deliver other women's babies, but never my own. If only we could have had more time, could have caught the cancer sooner, could have had a little Jonathan…but there is little point in agonizing over that now. Our children were lost before they were found.

Here I am, no longer part of two—I am just one, alone, and I will probably stay that way. Jonathan was my running partner, my best friend, my everything. He can't be replaced. When I lace up my running shoes on Saturday mornings, I know my run will be solo, always missing the man I love. But as I walk past Room 202, I can hear the unmistakable sound of that new father cooing at the precious bundle of pink. When I catch a glint of laughter from his wife, I understand that happiness still exists. As a neonatal nurse, I get to help bring some of that joy into the world, one delivery at a time.

Jonathan has left, but here in this hospital, I can still find a reason to smile, to hope. All I need to do is peek in that door and look at those three.

A Perfect Pinecone

The morning sunlight dances between shadows on the path ahead of me, a happy yellow glistening on the brown earth trail. I am surrounded by ancient trees that tower high, up to the clouds it seems. These pine sentinels guard the trail, soldiers of the forest, companions along the path. With hundreds of trees to my left and to my right, how could I be lonely on this solitary hike?

Peacefulness covers the land like a down comforter, so silent that I can hear my breath, my footsteps in the fall leaves, and nothing else until the drum of a woodpecker interrupts with a rat-tat-tat-tat-tat. Then two blue jays begin a shouting match, and the forest seems to come alive with noise. A wren chatters off in the distance; its cheerfulness lightens my step. The chitter of a family of chickadees echoes not far off, and the call of a wood thrush adorns the air. Something familiar is here.

As I trod on, the smell of the forest envelopes me. A vaguely sweet fragrance of decaying leaves on the ground mixes with the scent of pine. It is October, but the smell is Christmas, a thought that strikes me as bittersweet, and I feel a pang of sadness. A little shiver runs down my arms, but I shake it off like a cobweb and amble forward.

Through the shade, I continue my path, kicking my boots through fallen leaves until I realize a bootlace has come undone. Stopping to bend on the soft forest floor, I kneel beside the most gigantic pine tree I have ever seen. *What a strange photo this would make*, I muse. *Grown woman by herself, bowing below a skyscraper tree, hair escaping from under a bandana. "Wild Woman Praying to Conifer" could be the title.*

Beside my boot, a single brown pinecone catches my eye. *Funny how there's only one under such a huge tree.* I study it amid the pine needles. Simple. Unbroken. I've seen hundreds, probably thousands of pinecones, but this one draws me to it. Round and perfectly curved, well preserved; it must be newly fallen. I reach for it, feel its prickly edges, and hold it to my nose. The perfume intoxicates me, and in one whiff, takes me far away, to when I was six, the last Christmas before my father died.

A somber mood falls over me as I stand holding that pinecone, and I remember Dad. He had wanted the holiday to be special, knowing it would likely be his last. Despite his weakness from the cancer and the monster medicines he took, he insisted that we go to the woods just outside of Maysville. A family friend owned the land, always invited us to pick a good tree. Dad wore a flannel shirt that swallowed his shriveled body; Mom wore an anguished expression on her tired face. My brother, older and wiser than I, carried an air of independence as we walked in the chill from the car to the forest's edge that day. Johnny got to hold the saw—he was 11. I didn't have anything to carry and fussed about it. I whined unreasonably, "I'm not a baby." My eyes were red with tears; my fists were tiny balls of unexplained anger. Dad, trying to appease my tantrum and preserve the sanctity of the day, bent down and picked up a round pinecone and turned to me. "Here, Missy, carry this for me. It's perfect. Let's put it on the mantel for decoration." I swelled with importance at the gesture and held it like Eucharist as my mother and brother took turns sawing the trunk of our chosen tree.

A pinecone—that pinecone—was a bridge between my dying father and me that day. Maybe it was his way of telling me I mattered. When we got home, tree in tow, we were all worn thin, but Dad was fully exhausted. Johnny and Mom struggled to carry in the evergreen that had been secured to the roof of the car. Dad could only hobble in, apologizing needlessly for not helping. But before he laid down to rest, he crossed the living room with heroic effort and ceremoniously placed the pinecone on the mantel over the empty fireplace. He smiled at me and whispered, "Missy, that's a perfect pinecone. You did a fine job of getting it home safely."

Less than two months later, Dad was gone. Everything would change—in years, there would be a stepfather, a new home, more than a dozen holidays with an artificial tree.

The pinecone was tossed out along with the dry, brittle fir that January, only a memory now. But here, in this forest splashed with sunlight and shade, I have it in my hand again, and I know my father is with me. The pinecone that was connection, a link between my father and me, is a bridge still.

"Thank you," I whisper to the wind as I look up at the tree's trunk and branches. My words sweep away with the breeze. "I miss you, Dad."

I breathe a sigh, then head up the trail toward my car, toward my life outside the woods. Gently, firmly, I carry that perfect pinecone. It is coming home with me.

Sparkle

"Sparkling" was the word she repeated in her mind, over and over. The sunshine glittered and glistened on the waves all around her boat, her solitary vessel whipping in the ocean breeze.

Corinne knew she was finally free, as unrestrained as the waves, as light as the seagulls following her sailboat. Never did she dream she could experience this kind of liberation; still, she herself had cut the ties that had her tethered. *Ahh, freedom.*

He had been a binding rope, a stout cord—his dark brows and deep-set eyes were chaining forces; his strong hands and broad shoulders wrenched her back each time she struggled to pull away.

The marriage license she signed was in no way a license for him to brood, to demand, to confine, to take what was not given. Still, she seemingly had no power, no hope to slough off his manipulative hold. After four years, her wedding band was as merciless as a manacle. Three emergency room trips were followed by two social workers' visits. Still, she stayed, emotionally shackled, knowing she had no worth.

Until that last time, the time when his knuckles bled as he pummeled her, as he broke the skin on her back and thin thighs, places only he would see. Her four-year trance snapped, she broke from her paralysis, and with the largest kitchen knife from the block on the counter, she stabbed him until blood oozed onto the ceramic tile floor.

Out on the water, the fish must have appreciated her gift; they followed her sailboat, shiny bodies undulating just below the surface.

Her hair blew in the salty air, jubilation on her face. The last of the fish food fell into the green water, its redness turning the water a deathly brown momentarily, and she laughed.

Free. She was free. And oh how she and the waves glittered and glistened and sparkled.

Saw Dust

The boy tramped the woodland hills, flanked by a gray man in tatty flannel. Yellow leaves fell, sweet as baby tears.

"Slow down, Grandpop," the short denim bundle squeaked, bumping along the path.

The two stopped at a fence. "It says, 'Private Property,' Pop."

"Never mind that."

The two figures passed the sign together along a trail of cedar. Old man and little boy shared a gasp of excitement, breaking rules conspiratorially. The land was lush, the air electric with a vibrant coolness. Puffs of fog sighed from their mouths as human shadows and tree shadows blended and danced in the autumn light. On the wind they heard whispers of oaks. The old man spoke in a deep voice. "This forest land is our roots, James Allen. Our breath feeds these trees and theirs feeds us. You can breathe in their goodness."

The child looked up at his grandfather and took in as much as his lungs and his heart would allow. He believed it as much as a child could: These hills belonged to his grandpa and him, regardless of any old sign. These trees were their friends forever.

The sensations, the colors, his Pop's rough hand—they all whittled themselves into the boy's memory.

***

Time passed. Fifty years drifted from dawn to dusk. James returned to the hills a lifetime later, his turn to be gray and in flannel, an old man, flanked by a boy in denim. The child more interested in video games and text messaging, but still he walked alongside James, a grandpa desperate for connection, to share the woods and grow roots with his daughter's son.

"Private Property" proclaimed letters in black and white. "Keep out."

"Papa, we can't go."

"Yes, we can."

Beyond the old sign, a different land now lay—bare earth, brown dirt, sprinkled with wood shavings. Lifeless. Slaughtered trees had been dragged away, victims. Irregular stumps littered the hills.

"But-" the child spoke.

"But-" the old man echoed with a tightness in his throat and shortness in his breath.

The pair stood still, two straight silhouettes against the gray sky. One lonesome blackbird blew away on an aimless breeze.

"Damn."

Grabbing his grandfather's hand, the denim boy shrugged. "Guess it is private, Papa."

"Never mind."

They turned to leave. Old man eyes looked over a slumped shoulder a last time: where he had once seen life, James now only saw dust.

Fifth-Grade Project

Scowling:

She called on me in a contemptuous tone. I could hardly respond to the teacher's question since I was not listening. Instead, I had been talking during her explanation of how to do the social studies project, the litany of steps and instructions to get an A. My pal Terri interested me more than our fifth-grade teacher, Mrs. Major. In front of the chalkboard, her red eyebrows furrowed. She repeated the question.

Stuttering:

"I'm sorry. I don't know the answer." Mrs. Major pointed her painted fingernail at me with frightening disgust. *"Of course you don't. You were talking, Kathy."* Could have been my imagination, but it sure seemed she took pleasure in sneering.

Muttering:

"Yes, ma'am." Her glare at me, a chubby, underachieving 10-year-old, felt like a belt. Being pounded by her knuckly fist would have been easier than enduring her judgment. With tomboy fingers, Terri touched my wrist gently. Blood rushed to my cheeks. Tears brimmed over my dark lashes.

Whispering:

"She's a jerk." Terri was careful not to let Mrs. Major overhear. Terri, my desk partner, the one who shared my school bus seat, who spent the night twice last fall, knew my father was away at some weird hospital for people who like alcohol too much. He was gone, had been gone for weeks. She had seen my hands shake one Tuesday morning and hugged me tightly when I told her about the police who came to my house. Having a drunk dad is a sad kind of social studies project, I think.

Yammering:

Mrs. Major droned on about this home project, one that wouldn't take up class time, one that your family can help with. But home was chaos for us Smiths. Home was broken without my father there, just like it was broken with him around. Terri knew this, and compassion lingered with her touch. Thing is, Mrs. Major knew it too. Notes from my mother, forms from the school counselor. Guess she figured this is what happens to kids with alcoholic parents: they turn bad and talk too much in class and disrespect their teachers. They fail at social studies projects.

Sniffling:

I tried to wipe my tears and snot with my short sleeve. The class watched Mrs. Major as she pointed to the chalkboard, but they listened to me, twenty-two sets of ears hearing despair seep slowly from my eyes and nose. In the moment, I wanted to evaporate into nothingness. Mrs. Major couldn't stand the competition for attention. *"Kathy, straighten up. Just because your daddy is away doesn't mean you get to cry in class. This is fifth grade. Buck up."* My whimper became a sob.

Shouting:

Terri, the straight A student who would get to go to the gifted middle school next year, stood up, her chair scraping the linoleum floor. *"I was wrong, Kath. She's not a jerk."* Her voice was loud. A roomful of fifth grade eyes as big as balloons raised to Terri's plain face in shock. *"She's, she's, she's."* My friend paused, and at that moment, I knew Terri was as crazy as my dad. Silence. Resolve and defiance in Terri's green eyes. Then she found her words: *"A bitch. She's just a mean bitch."* Terri sat back in her desk chair, anticipating the severe consequences to come. A little bubble of spit on her top lip. Whoa. I didn't even know Terri knew that word. Blood drained from Mrs. Major's face. Students sat with mouths open, waiting for a response. The prim woman, her pencil skirt wrinkled at her hips, stood like a statue, caught in a moment of indecision. And then: *"Let's wrap this up and talk more about the project tomorrow."* Relief—Terri's, mine, the other students'. The bell rang a moment later. With full backpacks and empty lunchboxes, Terri and I and other kids scrambled out the door toward the bus line, that project completely gone from our minds.

Smiling.

Lock and Key

Through the tall hay, high as a pony's chest, I spotted him ducking. He scrutinized me, watched me silently. From my partial view, I could see his coffee-colored skin glinting in the sun.

Not knowing what to do, I kept to my chore, hacking away at the dead tree Papa cursed at all last week. Said he didn't have time to be hauling off some dead oak that fell in a lightning storm near a month ago. He told me it was a boy's job. My ax arm was hurting and sore; still I hacked. Every few seconds, though, I'd spy a sideways glance to see if that man was still there, hiding in the hayfield to my left. Not hiding too good, I might add. He must have known I'd see him.

What to do.

Only 13, I don't know what's right. Some say the rich folks should be able to keep as many slaves as they can afford. Papa says he ain't so sure. Don't really matter much to us, I suppose, since we don't have enough money for new shoes or leather gloves, much less slaves. Must be awful being somebody else's possession, even worse, a runaway. *He is gonna get hisself killed,* I thought to myself as I chopped at the limbs. Another sideways glance. *And he don't look all that much older than me. Maybe 20. Maybe younger.*

What to do.

My arm was dreadful tired, so I decided to chance it and take a break. Papa was off in town; Ma was making lunch. No one would catch me wasting a moment to relax my muscle. I'm not big like Papa, barely Ma's size, really, but I'm growing. Soon I'll be a real man.

Man. That black man. I caught his eye and lifted my chin his way. In that moment, everything stopped but the summer breeze. It brought some relief as it blew through my damp shirt. Then he lifted his chin too. *Not that much older than me, but bigger. Darker, for sure.*

What to do.

The man, he began to stand from the crouch where he hid. He was a head taller than that hay when he stood up full. *Geez, he really could get hisself killed if somebody saw him. Who knows what a person might do. Even Mama.* I thought of the rifle that stands ready near our kitchen stove. Here I was, and I had seen him. Who would see him next?

He lifted his hands through the golden-green hay stalks. Cuffs. Iron ones held his wrists inches apart. The man was locked tight by those manacles.

I paused, then looked at the heavy ax in my hands. I've never really been near a black man before. With a silent prayer we'd both be free of each other safely, I held the ax up and approached him slowly, crouching into the hay myself. No movement from the house; Mama had not seen me. Up close, the black man's breath was fast and loud. I could see whiskers on his jaws. His eyes, full of fear and pleading.

It took only a moment and not one word.

He put his hands near the ground, and I lifted the ax over my shoulder. The hay prickled at my arms and face. In one swing, it was all over. Using all my 13-year old might, the blade crashed down. *That iron chain weren't so hefty and strong after all.*

Free in one blow, the cuffs separated. His dark head nodded, he lifted his chin at me once again, and then he ran like a wild animal through the hayfield toward old man Carter's farm.

He had been locked. My ax was the key.

Free.

With a dirty, shaking hand, I rubbed sweat from my cheek, sensing one tiny hair poking from my skin. I'd never noticed that whisker on my chin before. *Maybe,* I thought as I headed back to the dead oak and my boy's job, *I'm gettin' closer to bein' a real man.*

Independence

As the youngest of eight kids, many moments of my childhood were milestones: last Baptism, last first tooth, last poopy diapers. Let's face it, I was special. Sometimes my parents appeared nostalgic about these 'lasts'; other times, they seemed eager to get things over with for the eighth time. In August 1972, the Sullivan family milestone was the youngest child's first day of school. Little Katie was starting kindergarten. Going to school sounded fun to me—my parents bought me new crayons, new lunchbox, new tennis shoes. Kindergarten was going to be awesome; I just knew it. It was practically as good as Christmas or my birthday.

I clung to my mother as she set out school clothes for the next morning, the day I had been gleefully anticipating. My chubby arms around her, she peeled me away and turned my round face up to look her in the eye. "Kate, this is a big step." Her words sounded like a goose honking at her young gosling. "Going to school, you need to become more independent."

Independent? What is she talking about?

That night, I had no idea what that word meant. I still didn't the next morning as Mom walked me across the schoolyard to my classroom. I followed behind her, watching her yellow sandals smack the wet ground. "Keep up!" she encouraged. "Stay under the umbrella!"

The heat off the newly soaked concrete smelled like worms, but it didn't bother me. I bopped along, pigtails bouncing, singing a made-up song about the first day of school. It was a jumbled tune cheerier than "Happy Birthday to You" and "Jingle Bells" mixed together. My lunch box swung in joyful rhythm.

We approached the school door leading to Mrs. Maddox's kindergarten classroom. Suddenly, my song stopped. The lunchbox stilled. Mom stepped over the threshold and into the school foyer, but my stout legs froze just outside the doorframe. "C'mon Kate, you're getting wet."

It looked dark in that hallway, and loud kids were all around. I felt dizzy. "You're blocking the door," a tall boy complained as he elbowed past me. My knees were weak; my hands got clammy.

"Mommy, I don't wanna," I whispered.

She looked at me impatiently. "Katie, I told you last night. You have to be independent." Mom grabbed my hand and tugged me into the school building. The ceilings were high; the floor was marble. Sounds bounced from all over.

By the time we got to the classroom, I felt tears prickling. When Mom led me through the busy room to meet Mrs. Maddox, hot drips were spilling down my cheeks.

"Katie, say hello to your kindergarten teacher."

I pouted silently behind my mother's ample legs, but I could hear the lady's high, sweet voice cooing. "Katie, what a pretty name. Shirley, she's your last, right?"

"Yes, ma'am. Now Katie, be brave. You need to be independent."

Still, I hid behind my mother. Instead of speaking, I began to suck my thumb defiantly. I was a baby, and I didn't care who knew. My hand was wet with slobber and tears and a maybe little snot, too. Finally, I spoke, thumb in mouth. "I don'th wanna be indepenthent. I wanna go back thome."

We stood for what seemed like a year, me crying, mom coaxing, teacher watching. It went on and on. My thumb was now my best and only friend. This was not like Christmas, not at all. Mother raised her eyebrow and her voice with two fear-inspiring words: "Katherine Ann!" But I couldn't be "indepenthent", at least not today. Finally, the teacher spoke with resignation in her voice, "Shirley, how about you take her on home, and we can try again tomorrow?"

Behind her, I could see Mom's head nod. It was unthinkable: Mother was giving in.

Kids stared as we retreated out of the room. I didn't care. I had gotten my way.

It wasn't a milestone for the Sullivan family after all. Instead of my first day of school, it would be my last day of freedom. As we toddled across the schoolyard toward our house, Mom held the handle of my full lunchbox in one fist and my hand in the other. "Kate," she said, "tomorrow you better show me you understand what independence means."

I was getting an idea of the word, and I wasn't happy about it. I plopped my thumb back in my mouth, and we walked silently the rest of the way home.

The Time Capsule

Thomas hadn't expected to be alive when the town's time capsule was opened. He thought the Maysville City Council's idea of a stainless-steel box buried under the new park's entrance was a complete waste of time and money anyhow. He didn't mind expressing his annoyance, either.

"See here, Jones. This is the problem," Thomas Walker exclaimed as he stood in the Maysville main library that March evening back in 1972. He was younger than most in the room but spoke with the confidence of a town elder. "The council and mayor are more worried about posterity than they are about today. You just stated that fancy capsule is going to cost $345, and that is without burying the damn thing and putting a plaque on the stone entrance." He readjusted the thin tie at his throat. "Let's forget this time capsule nonsense and talk about what really matters—making sure our neighborhoods aren't destroyed with all these people movin' in." Several men in the folded chairs clapped. Two stomped their feet in agreement. "You know what I'm talking about, Jones. Let's protect our neighborhoods, not pack a tin box full of crap and put it in the ground." Thomas wiped his wet mouth as he sat back down.

Despite the cool evening outside, council members took to mopping their foreheads with handkerchiefs; the mayor's wife used a pamphlet to fan herself. Thomas had, it would seem, turned up the heat. Nonetheless, the council voted that night 6-5 to continue with the time capsule. "You're gonna regret this," Thomas sputtered at the portly, gray-haired mayor as he departed the boiling library. The mayor shook his head silently and watched the young man pass.

Thomas returned to his little home incensed. As he lay in bed that night, clad in t-shirt and boxer shorts, he chewed on angry thoughts: *How dare Jones and the rest of the council allow this stupid time capsule. Don't they see that their efforts are needed elsewhere? Don't they know that Maysville First Federal granted two loans to colored folk last month? Don't they see houses going up for sale in Fox Brook and Pleasant Meadows? Those damn coloreds will be taking over half of the north side of Maysville if somebody doesn't stop them.* That night, alone in his little slab house, Thomas vowed revenge on the council.

"I'll show them," he muttered to himself as Thomas stepped out into the spring air the next morning, lunch box in hand.

His first job was to get on the time capsule committee, which could have been difficult after his challenging the concept of the project itself. Luckily, he knew the mayor's secretary, an awkward young thing Thomas had taken to the fall formal their junior year of high school. Mary obliged his request without question. He had skipped lunch to chat her up, but the bologna sandwich would wait till after work.

A week later, the committee met. With only six people in the group, Thomas Walker knew he could get his way. His confidence soared as he recommended they establish a chair and nominated himself. Tired housewives and retired old men were no match for his ambition. In only three meetings, the group had completed the requisition forms for the steel box and plaque, determined the contents of the time capsule, and proposed what day to have the celebration and interment of the box. Thomas' leadership proved effective. Mrs. Wilcox even brought him a custard cake at the last meeting, remarking how much Thomas reminded her of her own son Bill, who had died near Saigon at the hands of that yellow Mr. Charlie.

Late that April, the capsule was ready. At the entrance of the town's newest park, the mayor stood before a terrific group of citizens and business leaders, ribboned shovel in hand. He offered a long-winded oration on the importance of community and the value of Maysville's parks. He spoke of the past, of the future, of the time capsule that would be opened in fifty years. Thomas stood beside the mayor but did not offer any salutations of his own, despite his committee chair status.

"Let these newspapers, these school yearbooks, these photographs be symbols of goodwill to our future children and grandchildren. Let the road maps included here be a sign of the growth our fair town will enjoy this next half century. And let this most recent census list from 1960 show that these were the people who loved Maysville!" the mayor proclaimed in stately fashion. The silver box at the mayor's feet was already properly sealed for its underground home; the mayor, with other dignitaries assisting, prepared a hole in the ground large enough for the capsule. Kicking the last bit of dry dirt over the box, the mayor gave a jowly cheer and the crowd, tired from standing, offered an emphatic (if not quick) hurrah. People dispersed, the mayor shook Thomas' hand, and the deal was sealed.

The crowd, the mayor, none of them knew what Thomas Walker knew: he had surreptitiously included his own set of memorabilia in that time capsule. *The cowards,* he thought as he walked to his car. He was the only one brave enough to tell the truth, and boy would his contribution tell it.

For Thomas, like all men, time marched on, and life opened to him like a magazine, one page after another. Eventually he married that secretary to the mayor, and in a few years, he and Mary saved enough for a home that was a bit larger, in a neighborhood that was a bit more exclusive. Little Tommy came, and a few years later, they had Marjorie. The family went to church on Sundays and had picnics at the park. Their life was charmed: Thomas went from laborer to manager; his wife was voted PTA president three years in a row. But no matter the family's progress, Maysville was changing, and Thomas struggled to keep his cool as even their own neighborhood threatened to become integrated.

It was a bitter pill, but his wife encouraged him to be patient and have faith. In time, she had the audacity to suggest her husband try tolerance. She had learned from her efforts at school that things weren't always as one assumed, *people* weren't always as one assumed. Over the years, she tried to appease his anger and bigotry. Occasionally she even thought maybe she was getting through to him, but she'd been with him two decades and knew Thomas' stalwart views. She stood little chance in changing a man of such arrogance.

And then one May, Marjorie came home from college with a pronouncement that would rattle Thomas to his very core. "I'm pregnant, Daddy." She was a business major who had not minded her own business. Her father was, in a word, enraged.

"I won't have any part in this, young lady!" he growled. "Hmmph! Young lady, my ass!" Thomas tossed his newspaper across the kitchen table and stormed out of the kitchen.

His wife, though, had had enough of Thomas' narrow-mindedness. She insisted that Marjorie could live at home, have the baby, place it for adoption or raise it herself there, with them. "I will be right here for you," she said as she stood in the kitchen, late spring sun filtering through gingham curtains. Mary paused and then whispered, "Marjorie, darling, who is the father?"

"It's alright, Ma. I am going to be fine. Connor and I are marrying. He can graduate early with summer courses, and we'll get an apartment." Looking up from her seat, Marjorie looked into her mother's middle-aged eyes. "Daddy's never going to speak to me again. He won't ever forgive me." Her mother shook her head, trying to encourage her daughter.

Marjorie shrugged. "Mother, Connor is Black."

The wedding was on the college lawn, a law professor acting as minister. Marjorie's parents were absent, just as they were absent for the birth of their grandchild, Charlotte. Tom Junior, a man who loved his sister more than he feared his father, gave his sister's hand in marriage, and later wrung his own anxious hands at the hospital that November as he waited to meet his niece. A darkness enveloped the Walker home. Marjorie was gone, her pink bedroom untouched with fading band posters on the wall. Tom Junior rarely stopped by, only for a quick cup of coffee and usually when his father wasn't home. Sporadically, Mary tried to talk to her husband about forgiveness, but his quick anger would always stop her mid-sentence.

One day Tom came for coffee and brought a single shiny Polaroid picture with him. Mary gasped at the image of Charlotte, sandy skinned and darling, two teeth behind plump pink lips. Tom left that afternoon with his mother at the door, clutching the photo to her breast. She stood at the front of the house, photo in hand, when her husband arrived from work.

In two long glances, the world changed.

Thomas stared into his wife's wide eyes, then at the picture she held out for him. All the air in the man's pompous chest escaped in a fraught silence. He had been wrong. So damn wrong.

Forgiveness is a two-way road, and both Thomas Walker and Marjorie Walker Smith navigated it carefully. Connor Smith entered into the arrangement with aplomb, having already had a lifetime of experience dealing with bigotry and judgment. Mary was elated—her family was restored, with little Charlotte connecting them all.

Thomas' evolution was not perfect nor was it consistent. His path to understanding differences and respecting them was circuitous at best. Mary learned too. As long as they leaned in to love Charlotte, they would find the way, and they did.

The community of Maysville witnessed Thomas and Mary growing on the inside, just as they saw that little tawny-skinned girl growing on the outside. Charlotte was a frequent visitor to her grandparents' house, riding her bike down the sidewalk, practicing field hockey on the front lawn. Charlotte and her Grandpa Thomas talked baseball and shared pints of ice cream. They teased each other good-naturedly and made bad jokes. Charlotte did not know Thomas, the bigot; she only knew Thomas, the kind grandfather. They were best friends.

To his own amazement, Thomas slowly became a staunch supporter of civil rights. He saw how many people treated Charlotte and recognized himself in their ugliness. Some on their street raised eyebrows when Thomas, now an old man, staked a "Black Lives Matter" sign by his mailbox. He didn't care, though. *It's 2022, by damn. I should have put it up sooner.*

Fifty short years had come and gone for the Walkers and for the town. Thomas and Mary were wrinkled and gray but still very much alive. They had seen heartbreaks and happiness; they had changed with the world as best they could.

And then, it was time. A representative from the Maysville City Council had a brilliant idea: let the original chairman of the Maysville 1972 Time Capsule Committee be the one to open that stainless steel box.

When Thomas got the call, he feigned hard of hearing, but Mary, listening to the conversation, put the phone on speaker. Why of course Thomas would love to come and join in the fun, Mary said loud enough for the woman on the phone to understand. Saturday at 1. When Thomas ended the call, Mary exclaimed, "Oh, we have to tell the kids! And Charlotte can bring that sweet new boyfriend of hers!" She rushed to start the planning.

Thomas glumly sat down at his old recliner. His face went a deathly white. What will I do? His heart thumped; his cheeks sagged. Oh dear heavens.

He had six days to stew over it, during which he weighed a million ideas to get out of the event. Thomas had considered the city council cowards so long ago. *Now who is the coward?* he asked himself. He knew he had to own up to what he had done to the time capsule fifty years ago, but at what cost?

That Saturday, a crowd gathered by a table at the park entrance. Along with council members, there were parents and children from the neighborhood, a handful of news people with cameras and video equipment, even a couple of teens with funny-colored hair who said they were covering the story for their high school newspaper. Tom Junior couldn't make it because of out-of-town plans, but Marjorie and Connor were there, holding hands, Black skin and White skin clasped together happily. Charlotte brought her new young man. She was so proud to introduce him to Grandpa Thomas.

All Thomas could do was hang his head in imminent shame.

The emcee for the afternoon, a man named Councilman Holly, introduced Thomas and made mention of the Walker family members present. The group watched as two men in yellow jackets dug into the ground. When they hit metal, everyone clapped. In the work of a few minutes, the steel box was pulled out of the dirt and set upon the table. It took more strength than Thomas had to pry the slide lock open, but when a park worker managed, he backed away for Thomas to do the official opening of the lid.

A lump settled in the old man's throat, right above where his thin tie hung. There was no way out now.

The crowd moved in to catch a look at the contents, but a councilwoman raised her voice to suggest they give Mr. Walker some room.

"Fifty years," Thomas choked out, "is a long time. A lot has changed in those five decades. I have changed a lot in those five decades. We have learned to be better. To understand each other. Differences don't matter as much as they used to."

The people stopped looking at the metal box and instead beheld the man speaking. One mother said out loud, "That's right" in support. A few in the crowd clapped.

Thomas, full of fear and embarrassment, half spoke. "I made, I made," he stuttered. "Mistakes."

Councilman Holly saw that Thomas was faltering, so he swooped in to assist. "Let's see what you have there, Mr. Walker. He reached into the metal box and gently lifted newspaper. "Editions of the *Maysville Times* from April 1972!" The crowd seemed impressed. Thomas stood still, so the councilman continued. "Looks like this one is a map of the city from fifty years ago!"

Someone in the crowd remarked, "I don't think they even make maps like that anymore!" The group laughed. Despite the April breeze, Thomas began to sweat.

The councilman pulled item after item from the silver box. It seemed like slow torture to Thomas, standing beside the table. He wasn't sure how much longer he could take the anticipation. In a short moment, everyone would know his secret, that he, Thomas Kilkenny Walker, had snuck an ugliness into that time capsule that would reveal him a horrible, hideous man. Mary knew how his heart had changed; Marjorie did too. But Charlotte...

"What's this?" spoke the councilman, far louder than he needed to. In his hands, he held a manila envelope with Thomas' own handwriting. "Let's see. It reads, 'Because you all need to know the truth.' Why, it's signed by Thomas Walker himself. Thomas, you sly man! What did you sneak into the time capsule? Is it a love note for Mary?" The group again laughed but the old man couldn't manage even half a smile. "OK, I am going to open it, unless someone else wants."

Charlotte, her dark hair shining in the sunlight, stepped forward. "Umm, sir. Could I? I am Mr. Walker's granddaughter."

Clapping erupted. "Of course, my dear. That would be perfect."

The few photographers present poised themselves for the perfect photo with Charlotte holding the envelope in the foreground and Thomas in the background. The crowd was enrapt.

Charlotte reread her father's cursive on the front. "Because you all need to know the truth," she spoke loudly, with confidence. She peeled back the flap and gave the envelope a little shake. Out came several yellowed papers. "Umm," she paused, buying a moment to understand. "There's a flyer here." She squinted her eyes, reading in the bright sunlight. "'No Coloreds Here,' it says. 'Meeting on Friday to discuss what our next steps are.'" The crowd made "Oh" sounds, not really understanding. A wave of nervousness rippled through the group. Charlotte pulled out another paper, hoping to make sense of what she was seeing. It was *The Crusader*, the masthead proclaimed, the national paper of the Ku Klux Klan. Her brown hands held it up for the group to see.

The people looked confused, repulsed. Then her eyes turned bright and with a smile she faced the old man. "Grandpa, you amaze me." Her voice seemed to tighten, a sigh in her throat. "'Because you all need to know the truth.' The truth. Grandpa, I get it. You understood fifty years ago that bigotry and prejudice were hurting people. You knew that Black people were suffering, that they couldn't always live where they wanted or work where they would have liked, even in 1972. Grandpa, you really are amazing. Even back then, you knew that racism was evil." In a flash, she stepped past Councilman Holly to embrace her grandfather.

He leaned into her hug with all his energy; relief came in his granddaughter's squeeze. As he held the young woman, the old man's eyes met his wife's, and she nodded softly. Would Thomas tell Charlotte the truth? Would he face his granddaughter with the fact of who he was fifty, forty, even twenty years ago? That was a decision for another time. For the moment, he just wanted to hold his granddaughter. The crowd cheered.

Thomas hadn't expected to be alive when the town's time capsule was opened, but he was indeed living. When that silver box was finally dug up, he discovered a humility he couldn't have fathomed as a bold young man.

The contents of the 1972 Maysville Time Capsule were boxed up to be delivered to the library for display and the crowd began to disperse. At his car, Charlotte hugged her grandfather one more time with a promise to visit on Sunday for dinner. Her new young man, dark and tall, reached to shake Thomas' hand.

"Thank you, sir. What an afternoon," he exclaimed. "I can see why Charlotte is so proud of her granddaddy. You're a hero." Thomas shrugged in embarrassment. He knew he was anything but heroic. He also knew he was damn lucky—to have survived the day with his family intact and to be a man who changed.

Katie Sullivan Hughbanks holds Bachelor of Arts and Master of Education degrees from the University of Louisville. Her poetry and narrative writing have appeared in various publications, including *Trajectory, Calliope, Making Waves, Ignatian, Bric-a-Brac, Kentucky Monthly, Kudzu, Pegasus, The Courier-Journal, Louisville Eccentric Observer, Sage-ing, Dodging the Rain* (Ireland), and *Flight Writing* (Ireland). Her writing honors include awards from Women Who Write, *LEO Weekly*, Heartland Society of Women Writers, and Kentucky State Poetry Society, and her first chapbook, *Blackbird Songs*, was published in 2019 by Prolific Press. In addition to writing honors, her photography has earned recognition from numerous literary journals, nationally and internationally. Hughbanks teaches English and Creative Writing at Assumption High School and lives in her hometown, Louisville, Kentucky, with her amazing and supportive husband, Dannis, their golden retriever, Peanut, and a cat named Ebby.